For Benoit and Liselotte

English translation copyright © 2014 by Skyhorse Publishing, Inc.

Originally published as *Der Schluckauf* and published by arrangement with Gerstenberg Verlag, Hildesheim © 2013 Gerstenberg Verlag, Hildesheim, Germany.

Sky Pony Press books may be purchased in bulk at special discounts for sales promotion, corporate gifts, fund-raising, or educational purposes. Special editions can also be created to specifications. For details, contact the Special Sales Department, Sky Pony Press, 307 West 36th Street, 11th Floor, New York, NY 10018 or info@skyhorsepublishing.com.

Sky Pony® is a registered trademark of Skyhorse Publishing, Inc.®, a Delaware corporation.

Visit our website at www.skyponypress.com.

10 9 8 7 6 5 4 3 2 1

Manufactured in China, August 2013
This product conforms to CPSIA 2008

Library of Congress Cataloging-in-Publication Data is available on file.

ISBN: 978-1-62636-387-8

THE HICCUP

Ingrid Sissung
Translated by Connie Stradling Morby

Sky Pony Press
New York

Sometimes when you eat or speak too quickly, funny things can happen . . . like with Elliott the bear who got the hiccups. And since the hiccups wouldn't go away, Elliott became very grouchy.

What made him especially angry was that his cousin Lutz, who was visiting him in the woods, did not get the hiccups and was making fun of him.

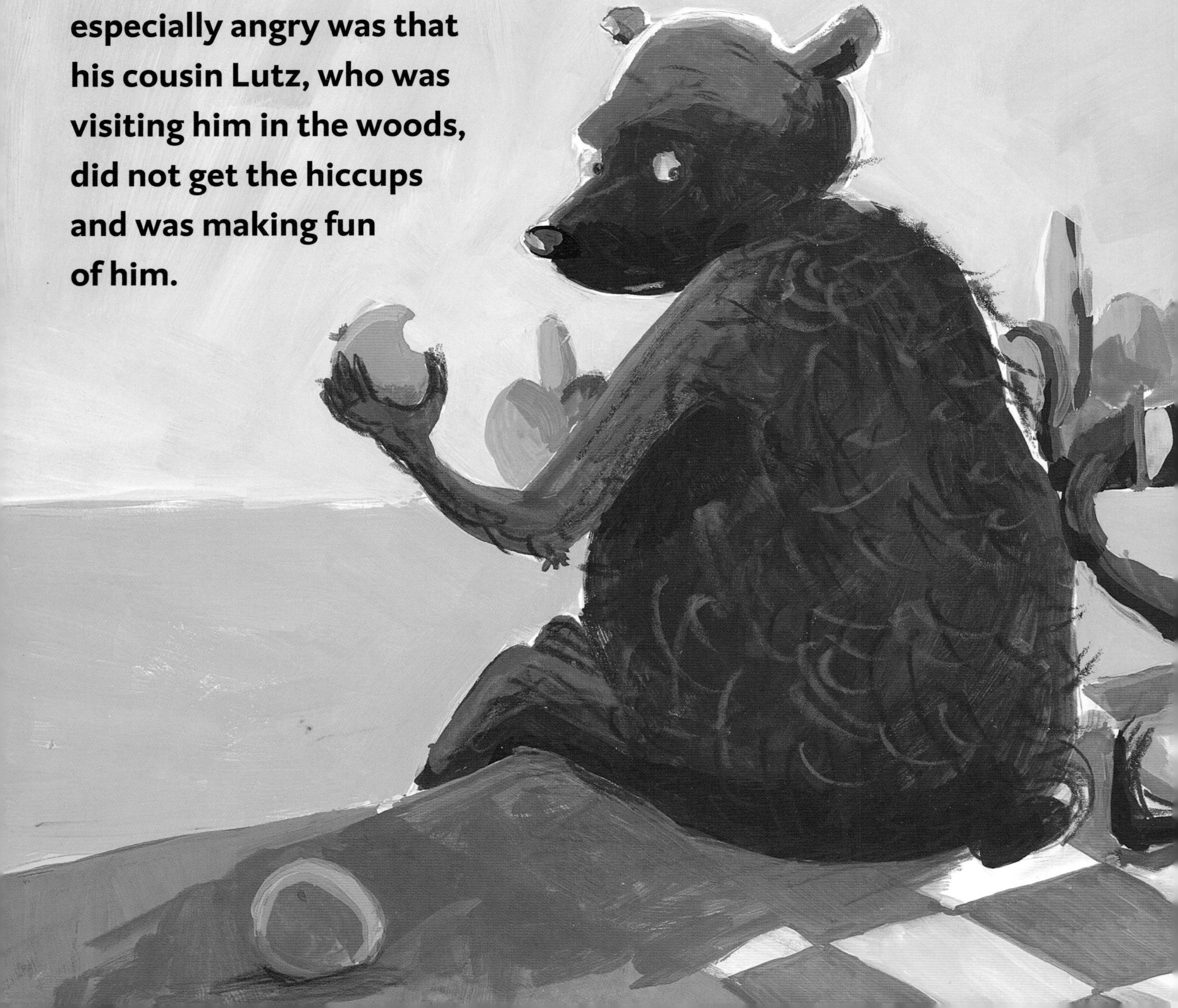

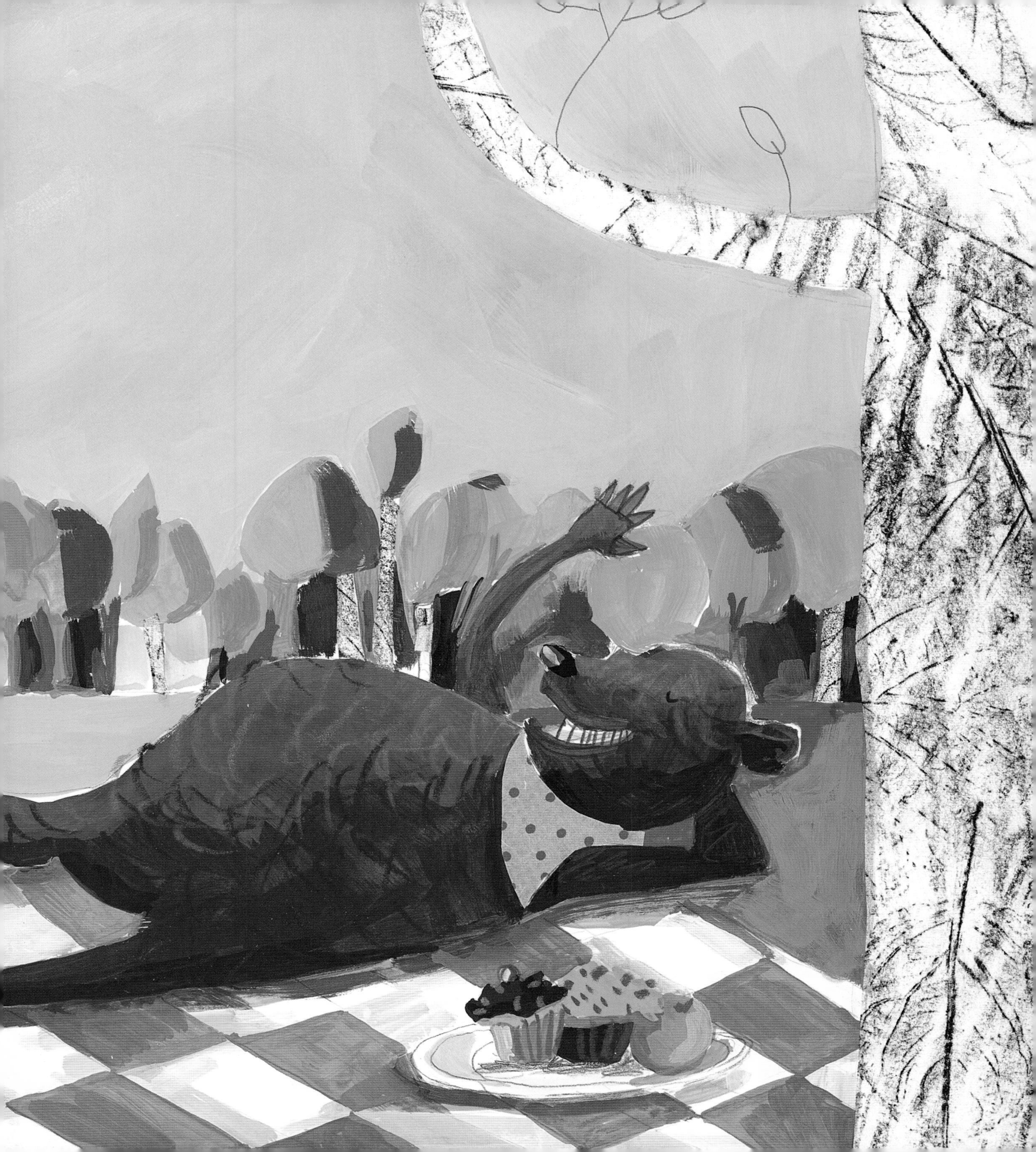

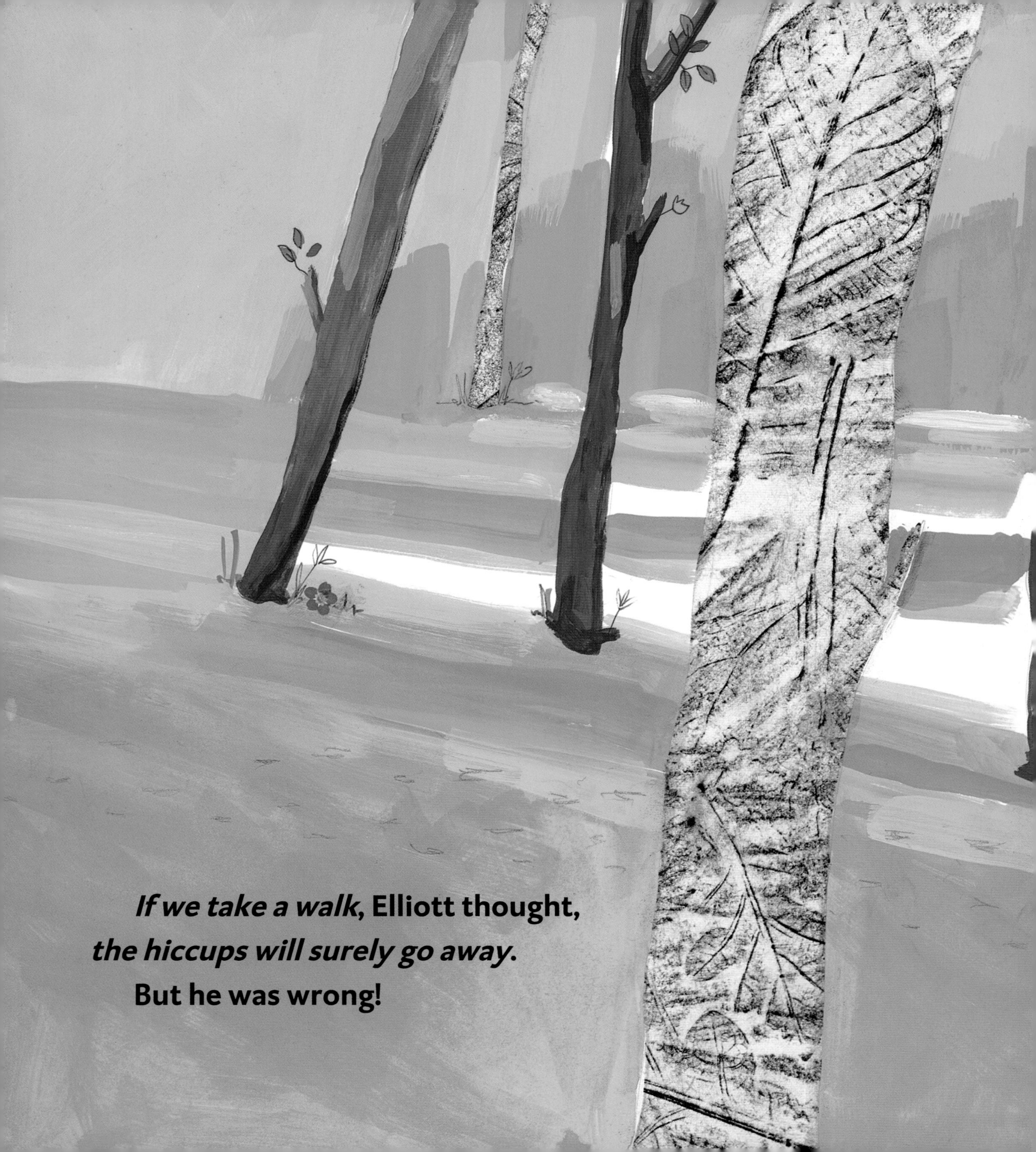

If we take a walk, Elliott thought, *the hiccups will surely go away*.

But he was wrong!

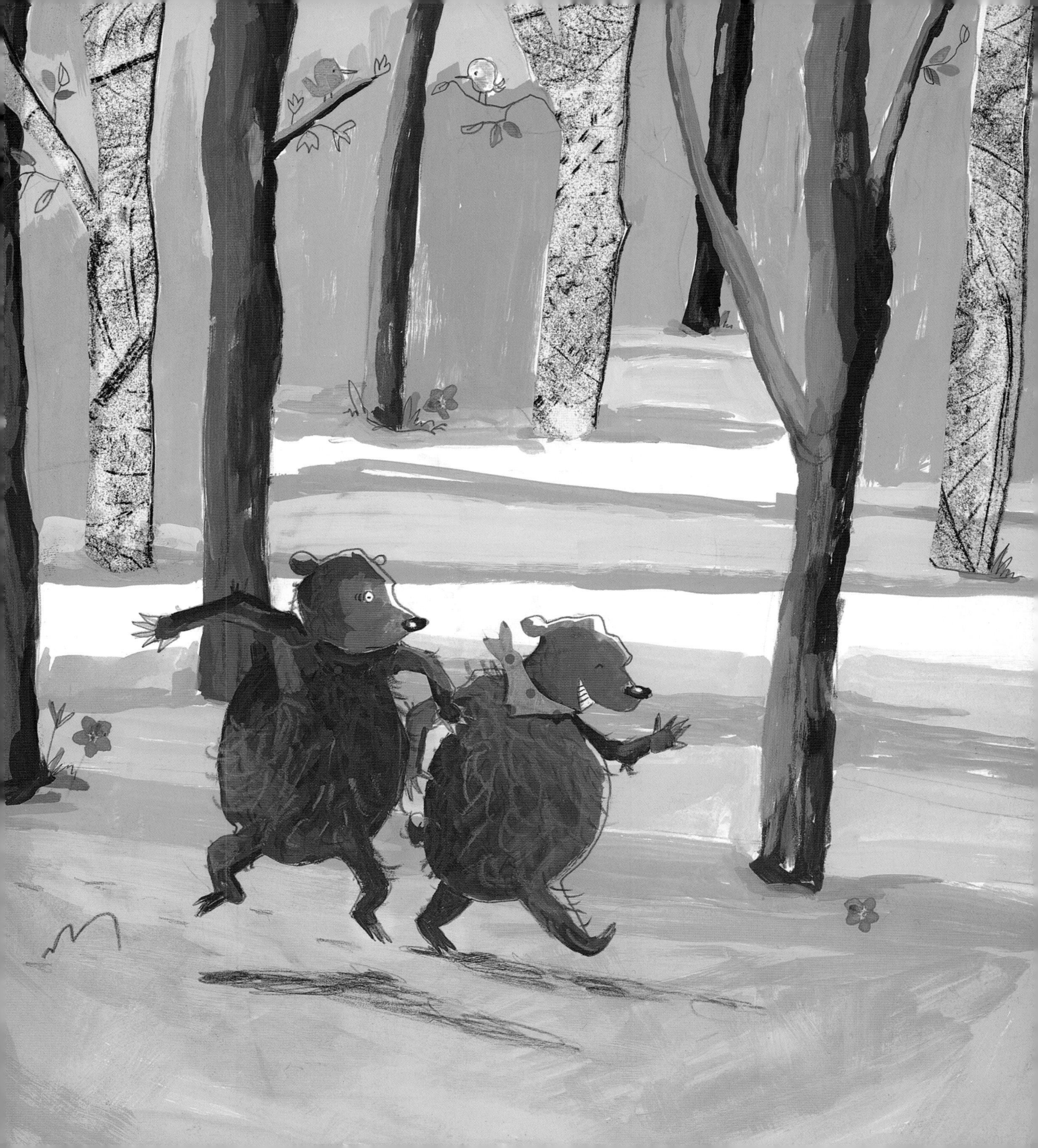

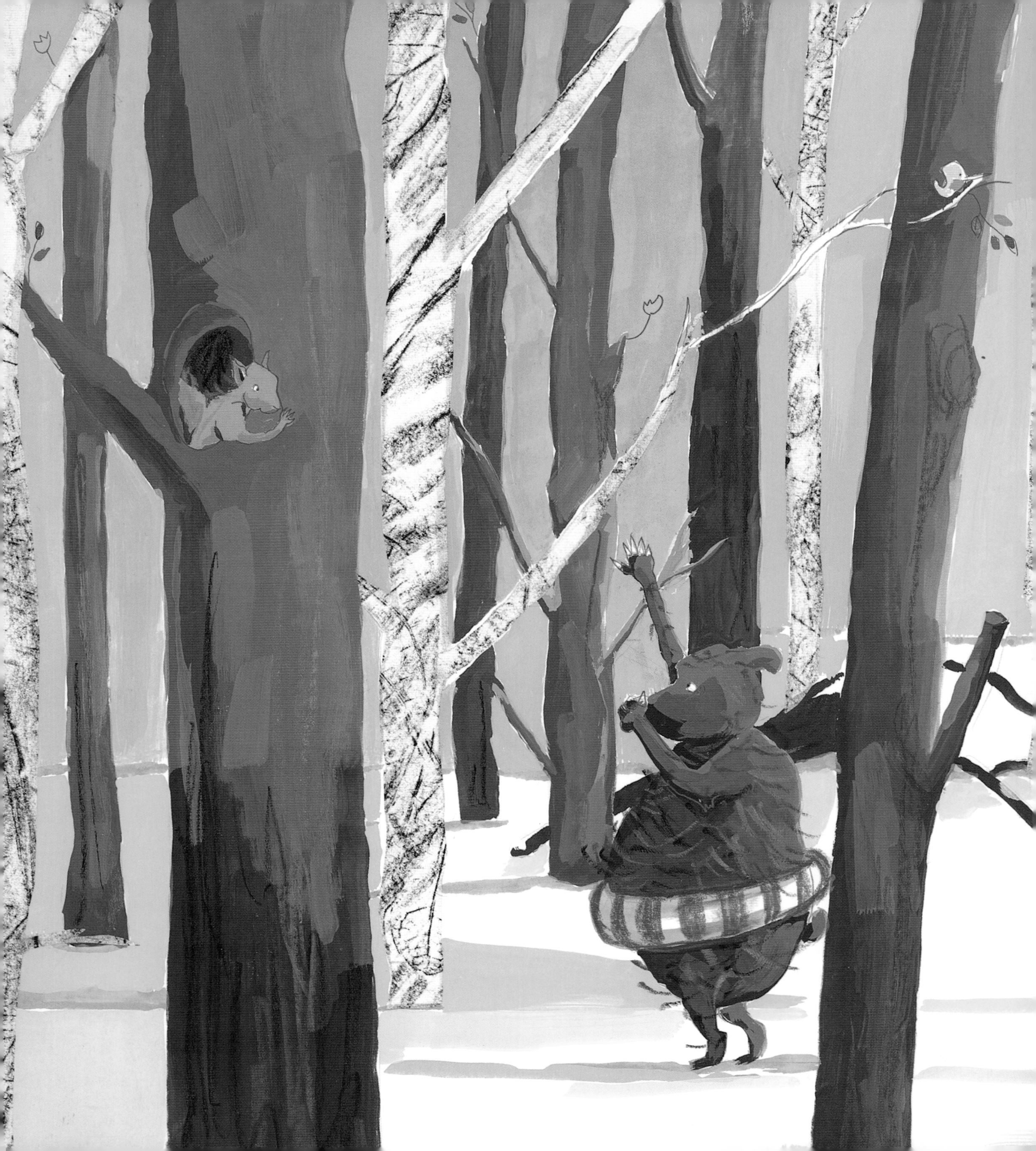

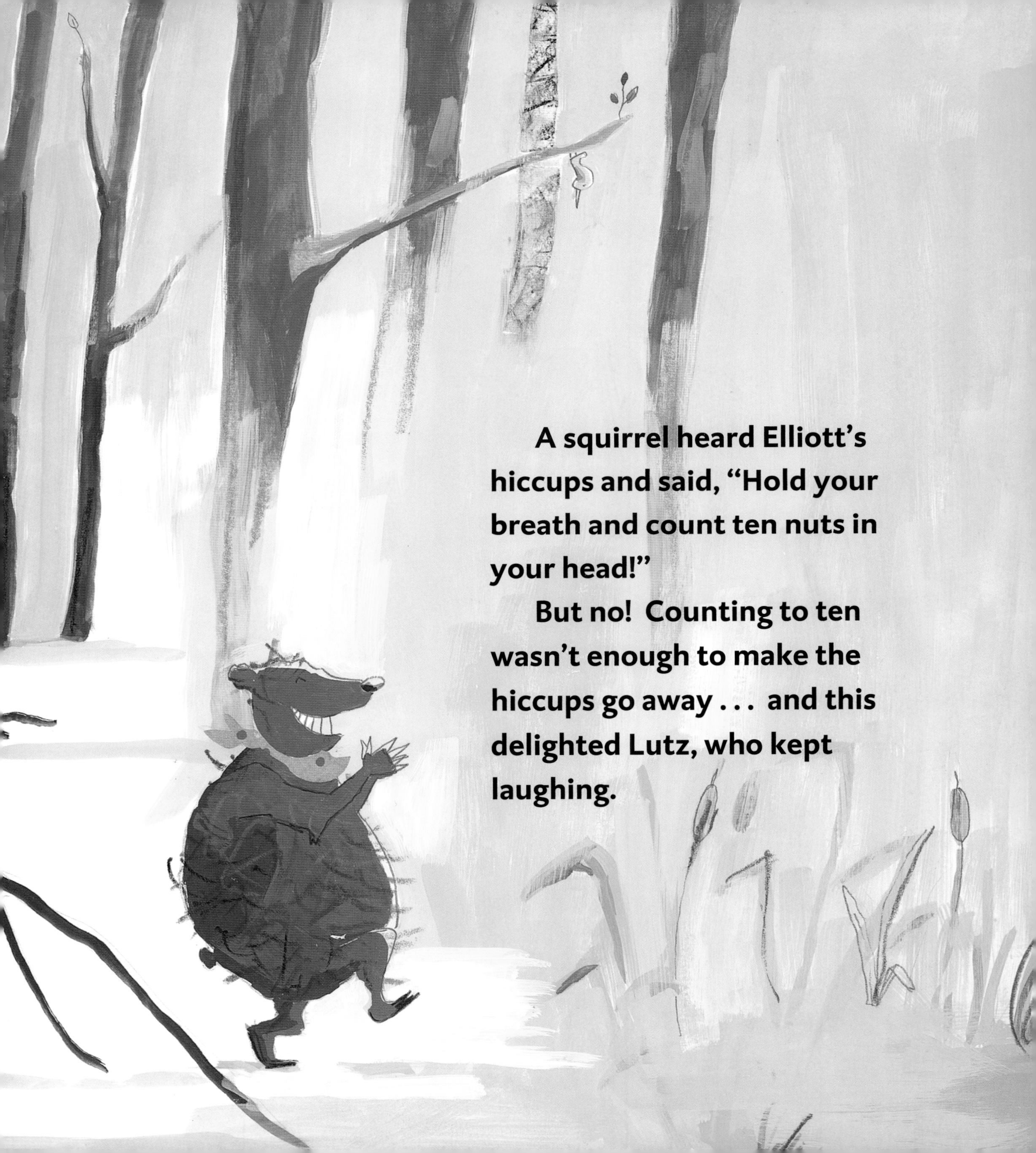

A squirrel heard Elliott's hiccups and said, "Hold your breath and count ten nuts in your head!"

But no! Counting to ten wasn't enough to make the hiccups go away . . . and this delighted Lutz, who kept laughing.

In a pond, a frog was hard at work practicing his swimming. When he heard Elliott, he said, "You should drink a lot of water all at once!"

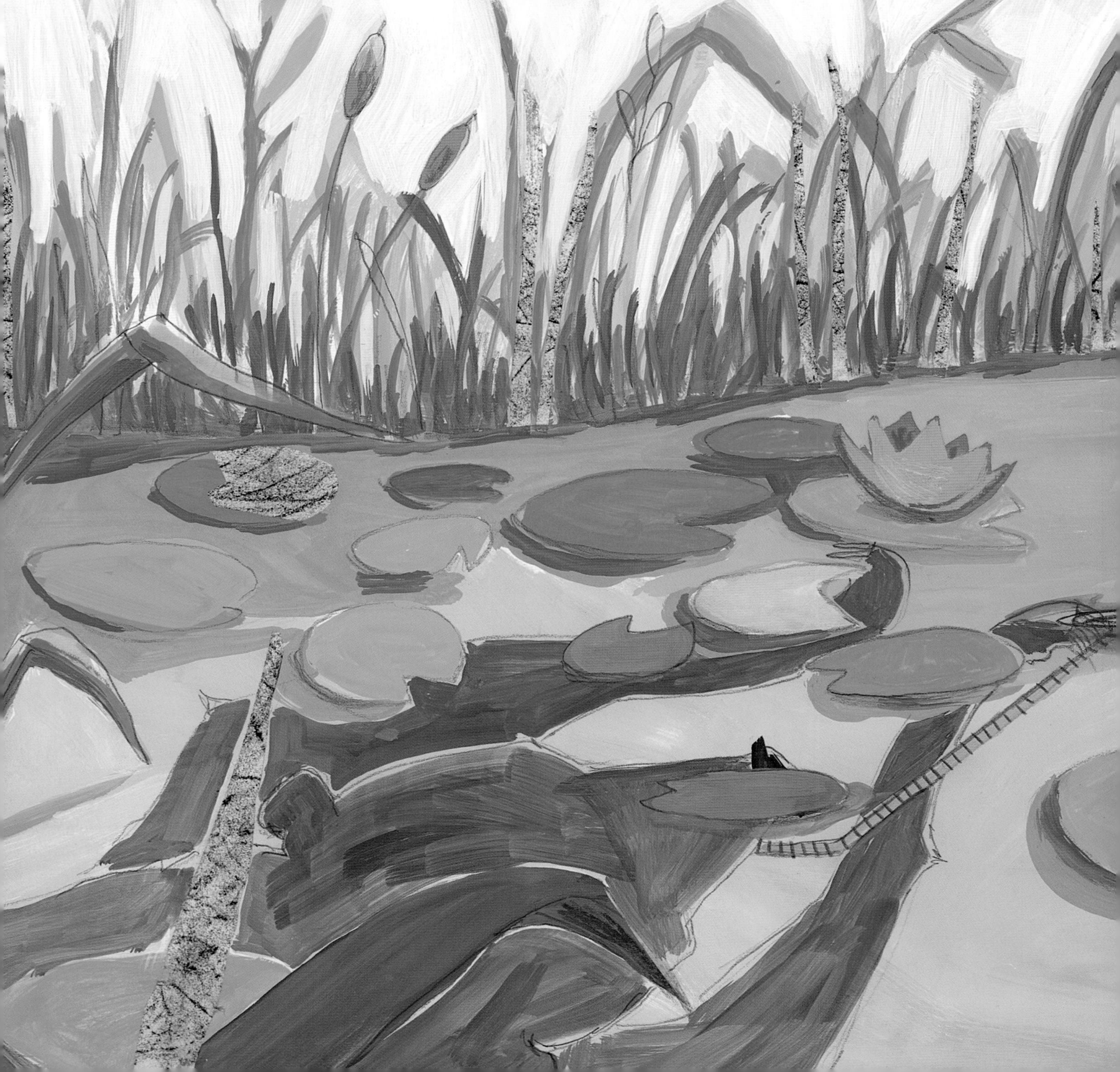

But no! The hiccups did not stop.

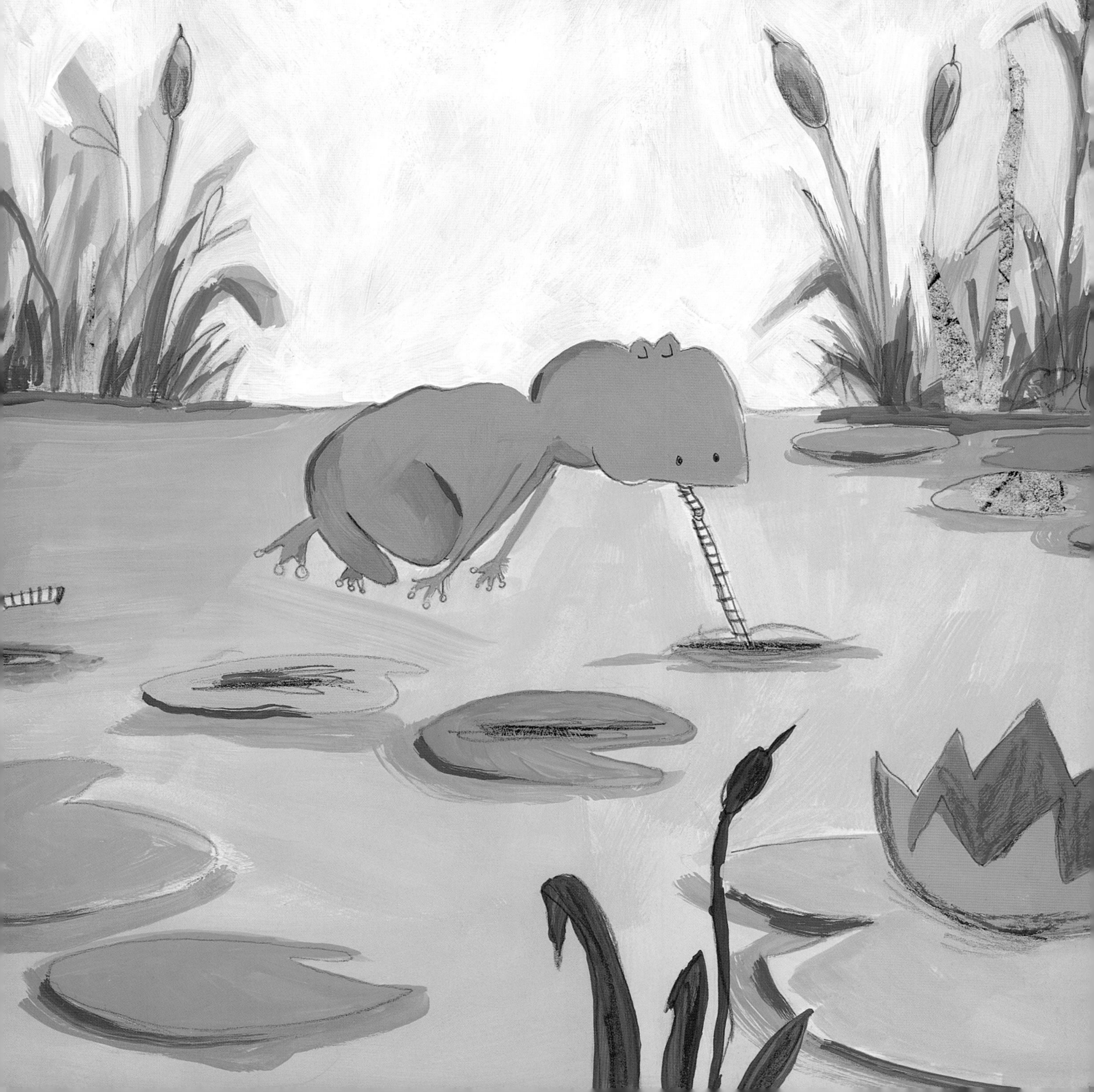

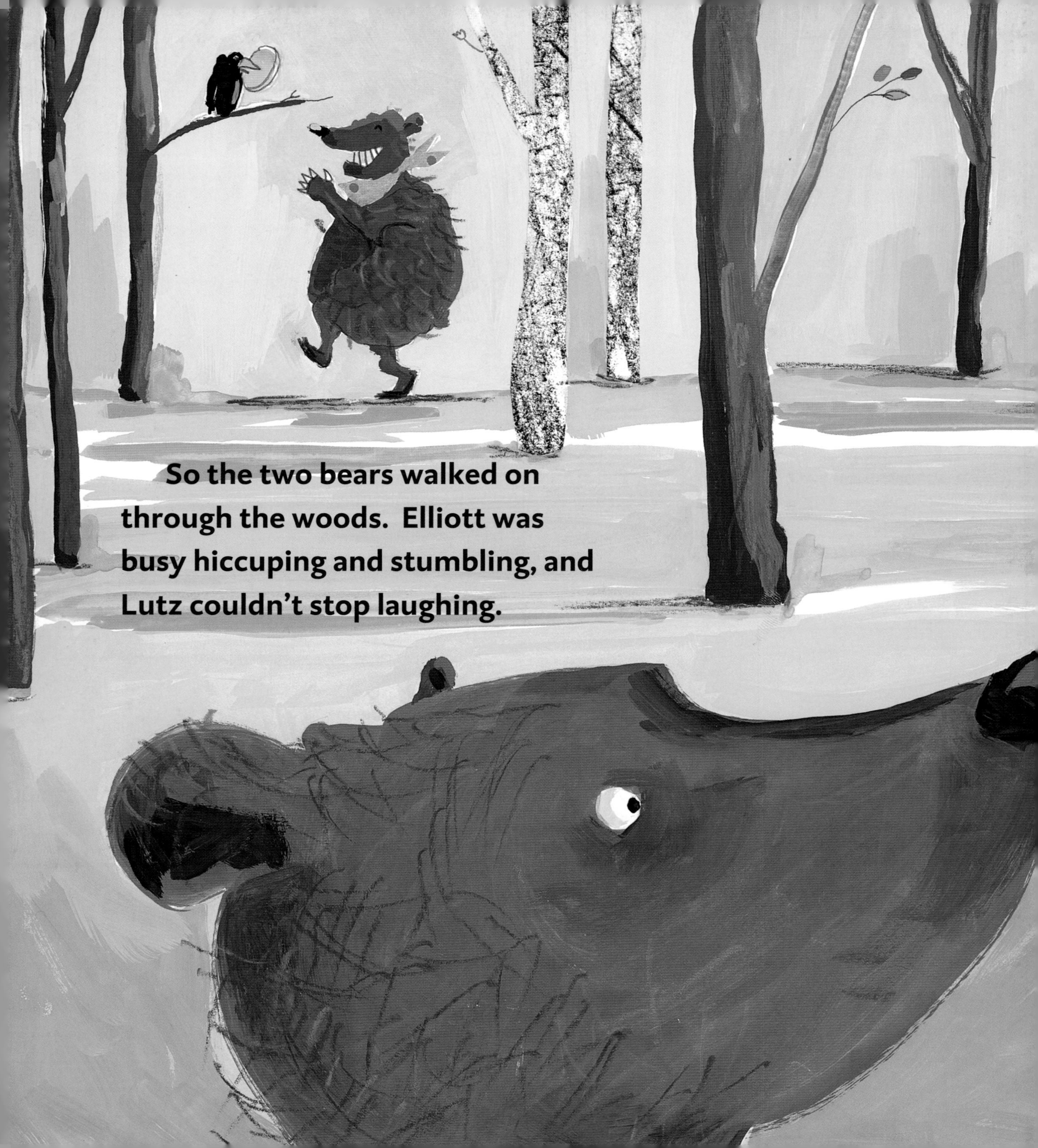

So the two bears walked on through the woods. Elliott was busy hiccuping and stumbling, and Lutz couldn't stop laughing.

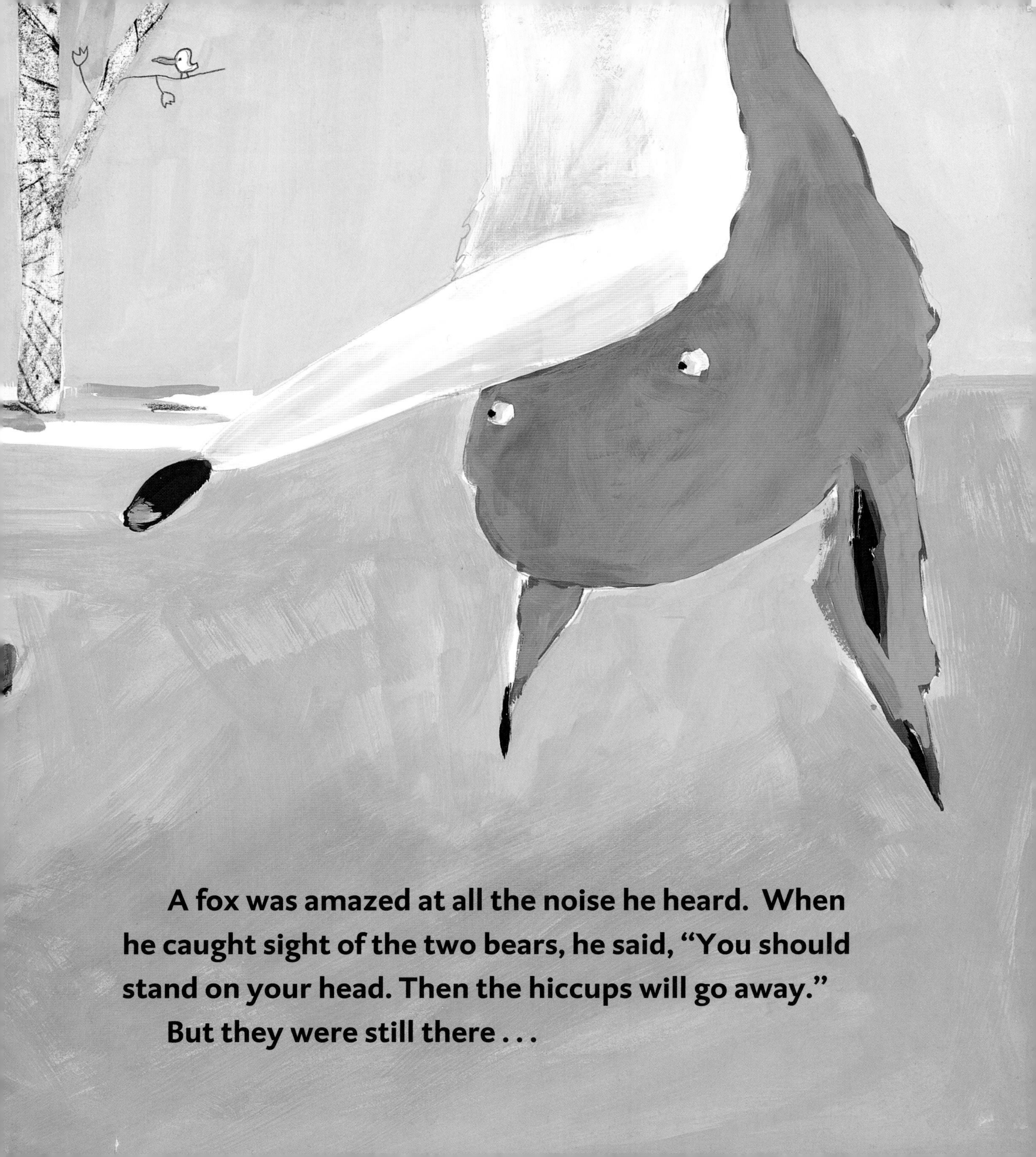

A fox was amazed at all the noise he heard. When he caught sight of the two bears, he said, “You should stand on your head. Then the hiccups will go away.”

But they were still there . . .

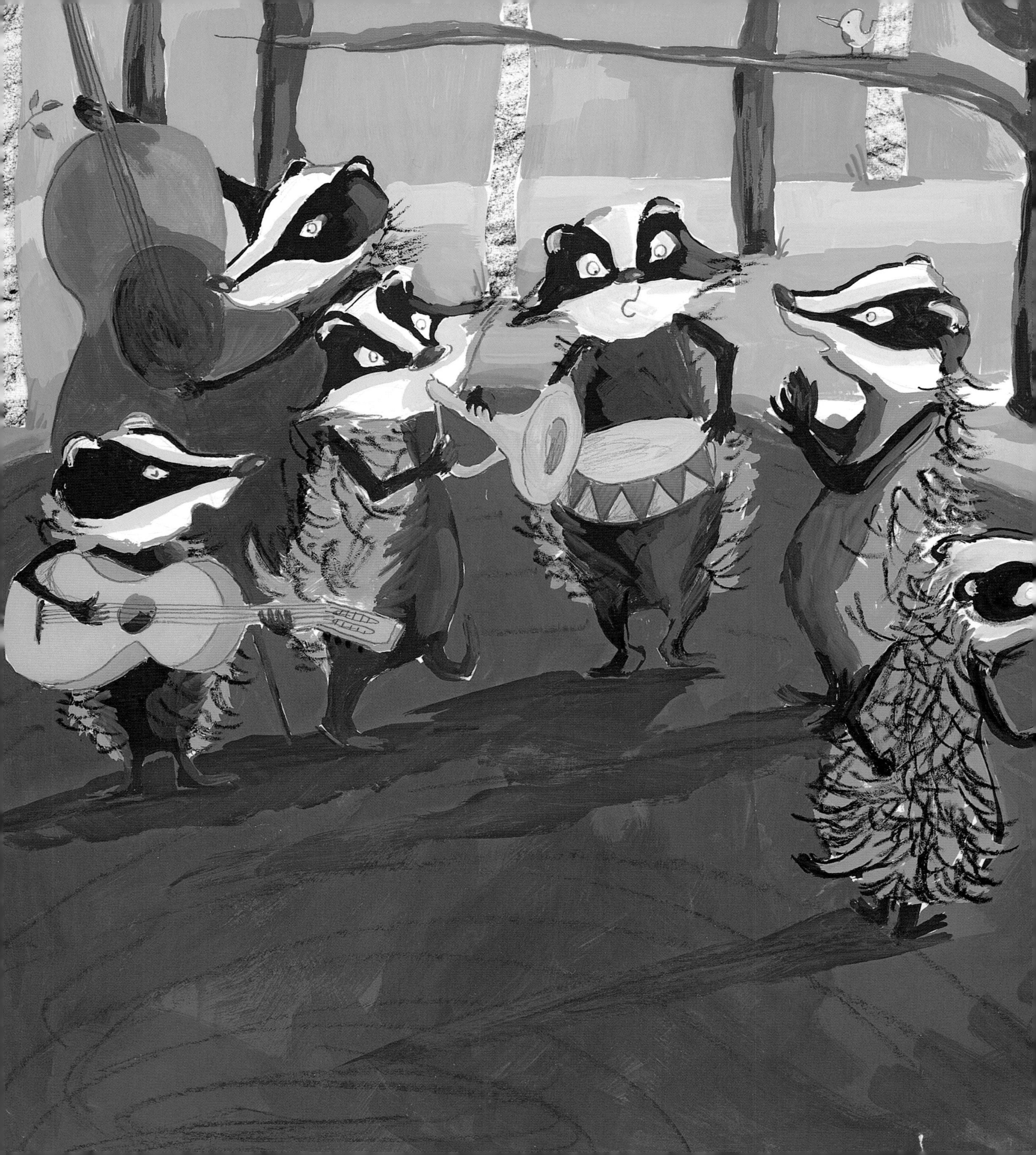

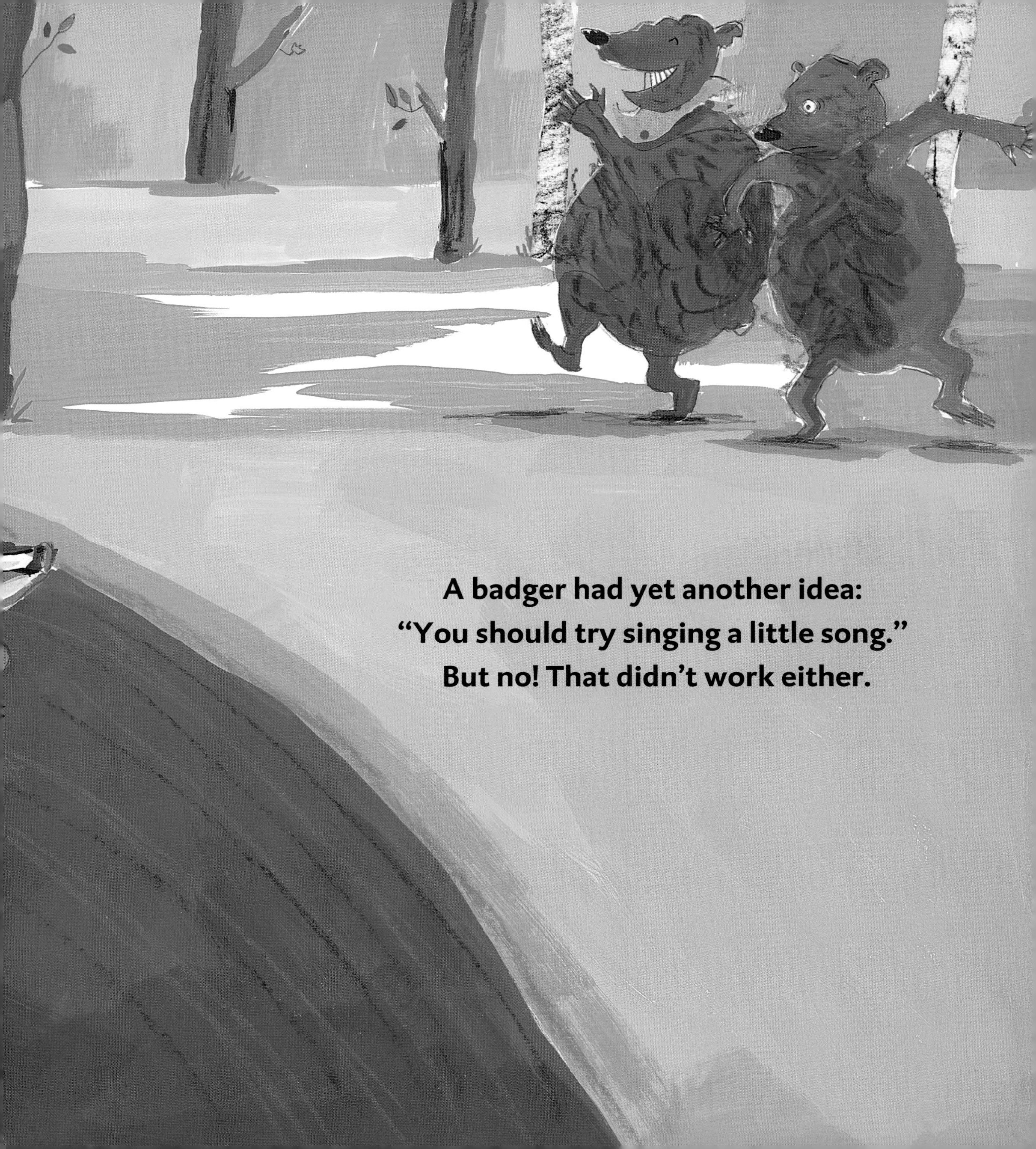

A badger had yet another idea:
"You should try singing a little song."
But no! That didn't work either.

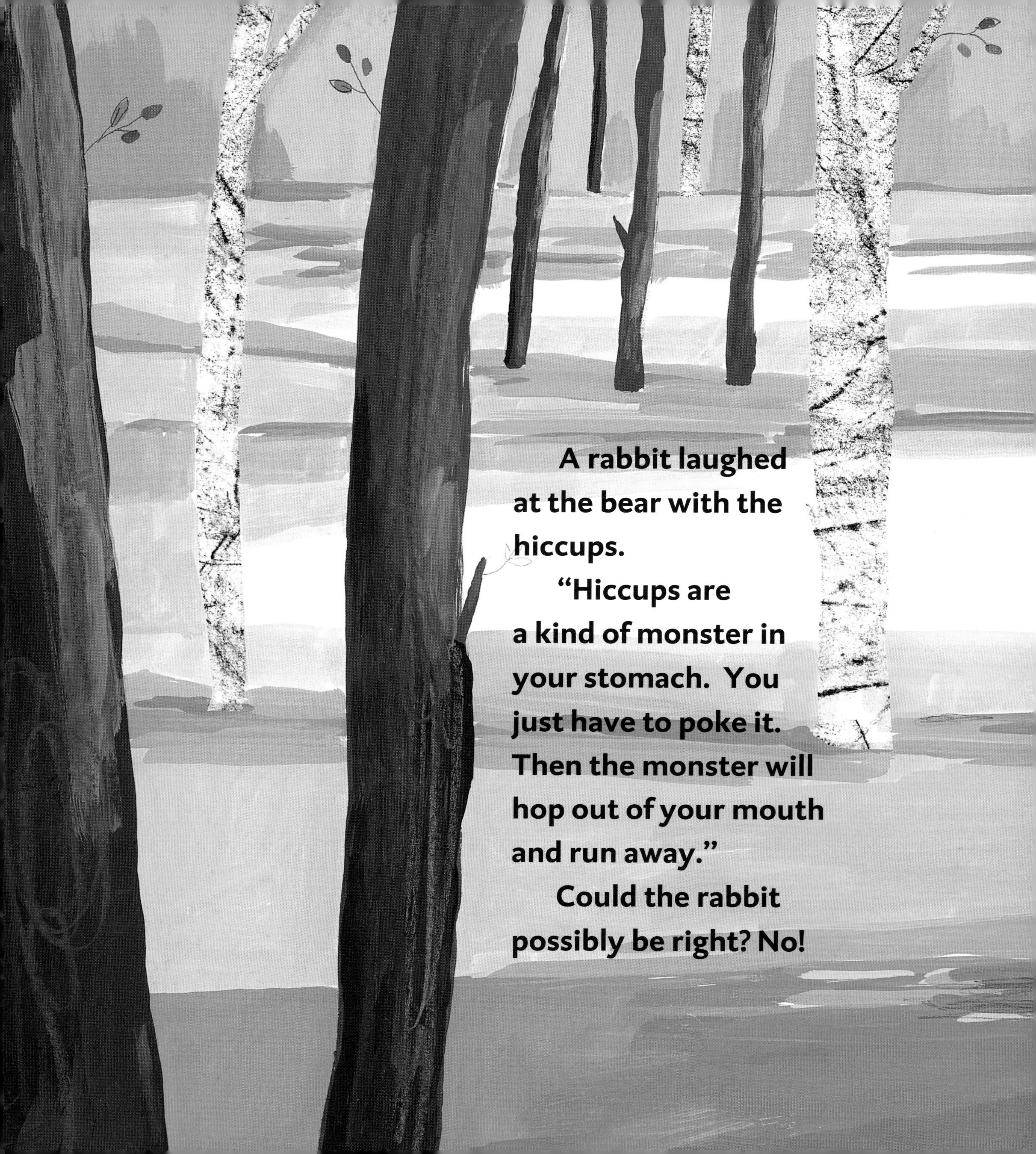

A rabbit laughed at the bear with the hiccups.

"Hiccups are a kind of monster in your stomach. You just have to poke it. Then the monster will hop out of your mouth and run away."

Could the rabbit possibly be right? No!

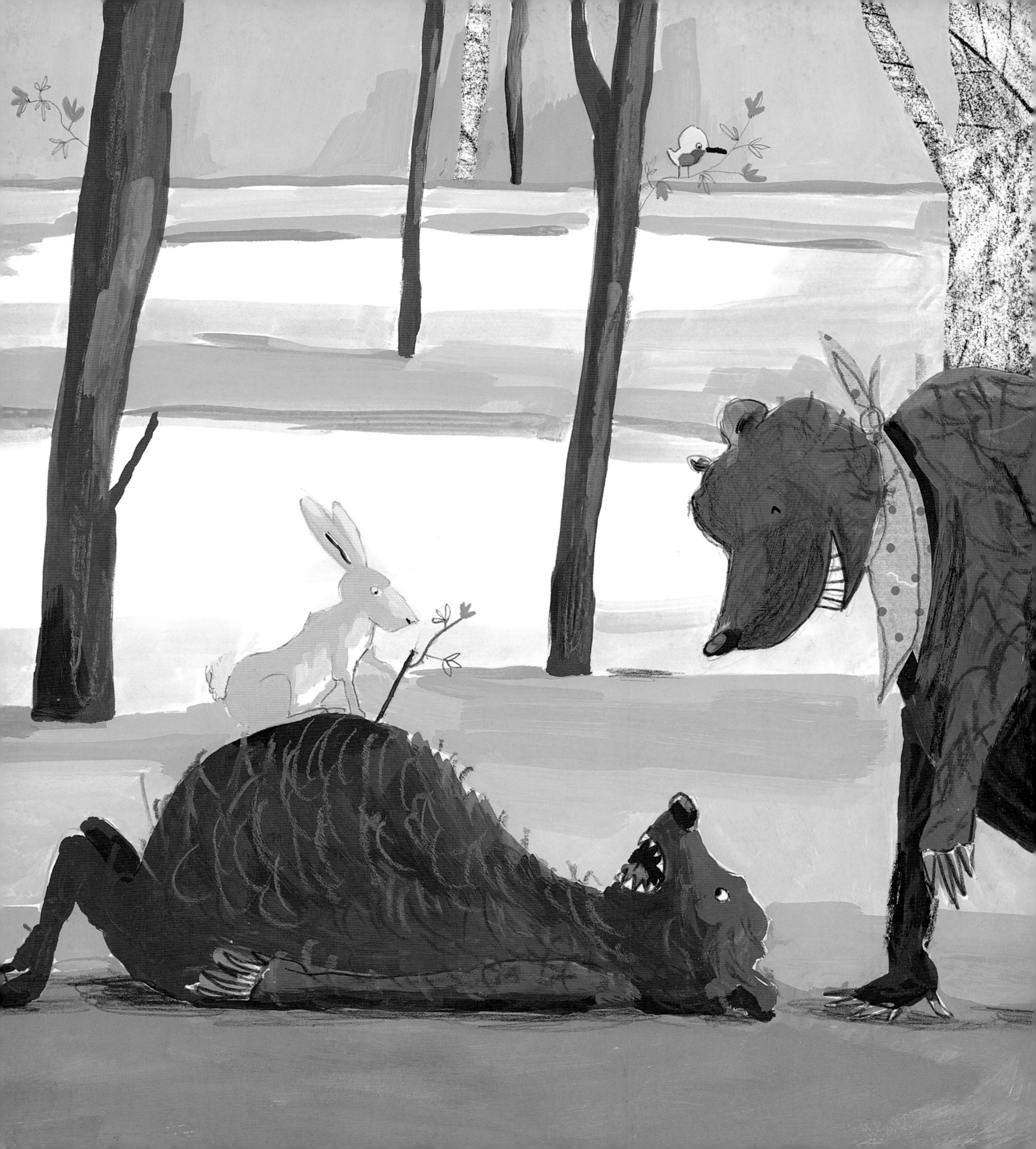

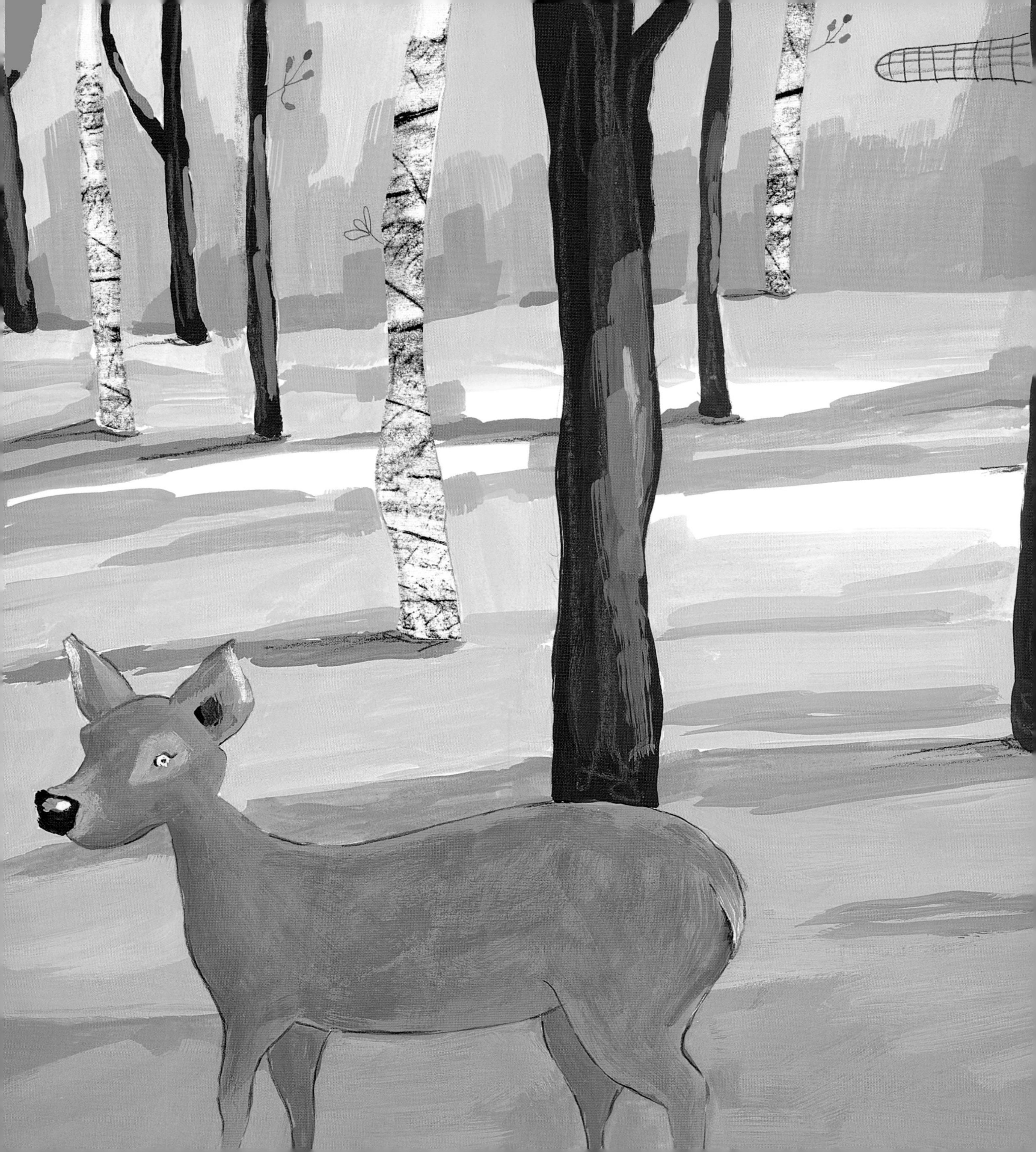

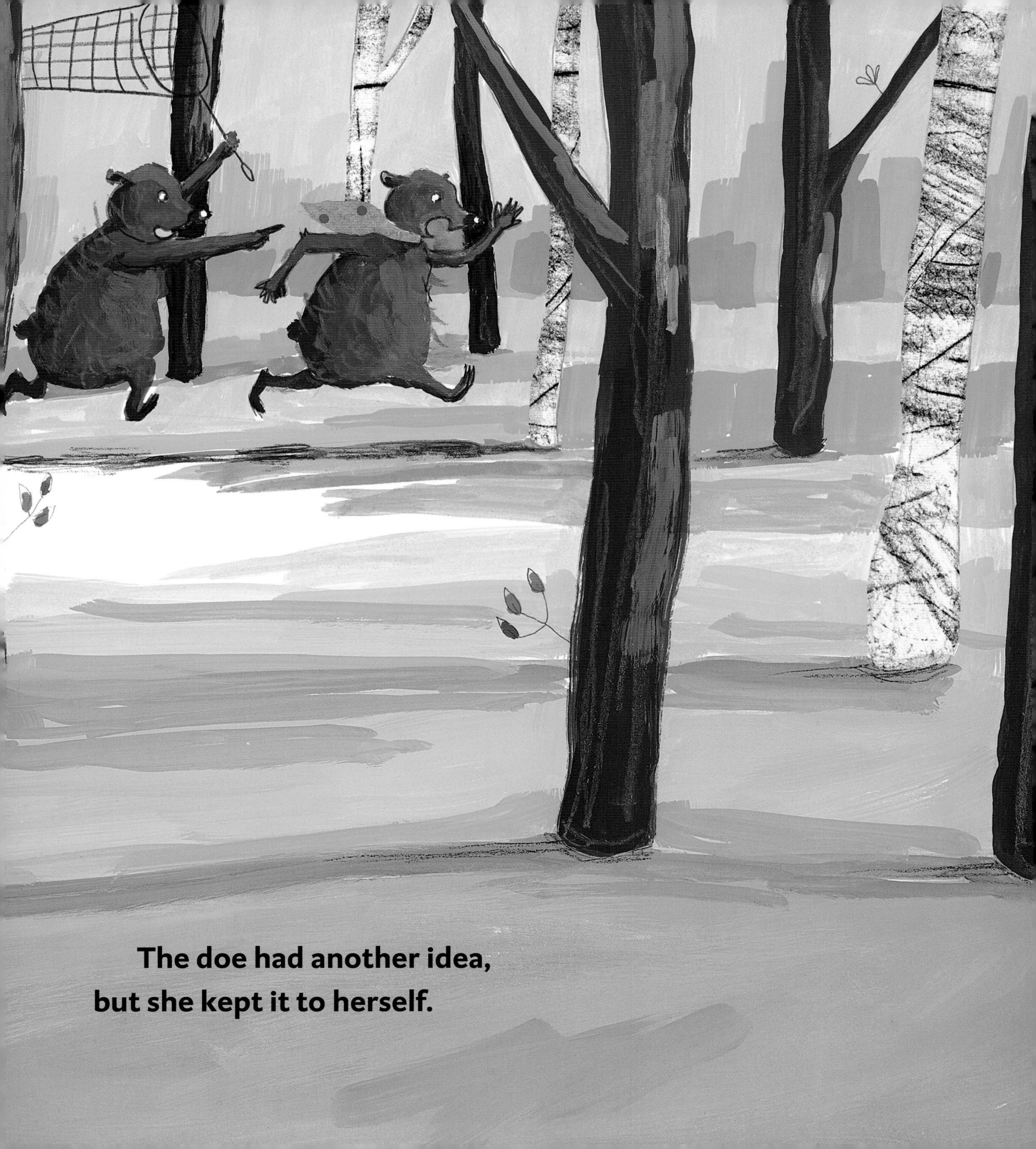

The doe had another idea,
but she kept it to herself.

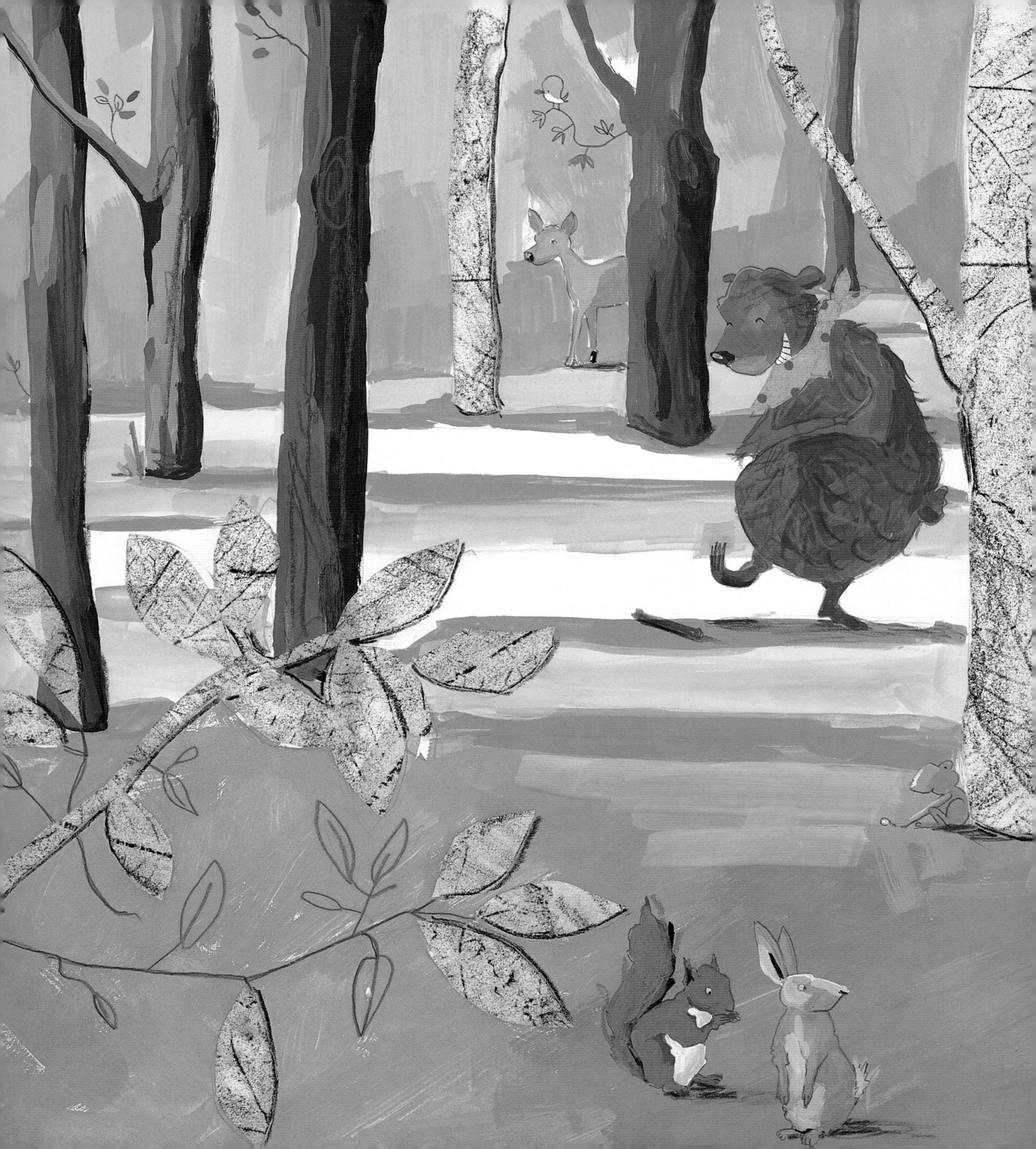

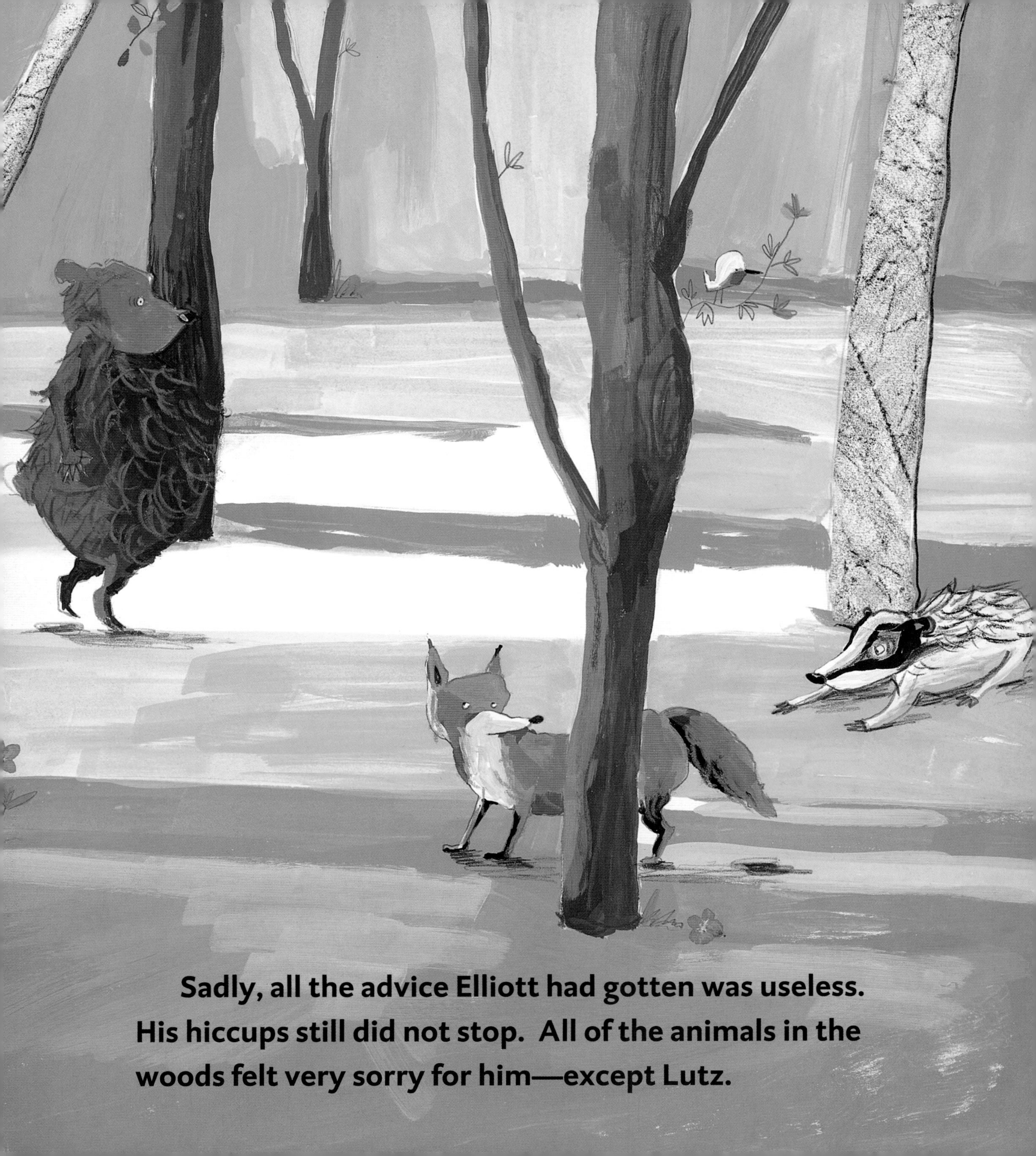

Sadly, all the advice Elliott had gotten was useless. His hiccups still did not stop. All of the animals in the woods felt very sorry for him—except Lutz.

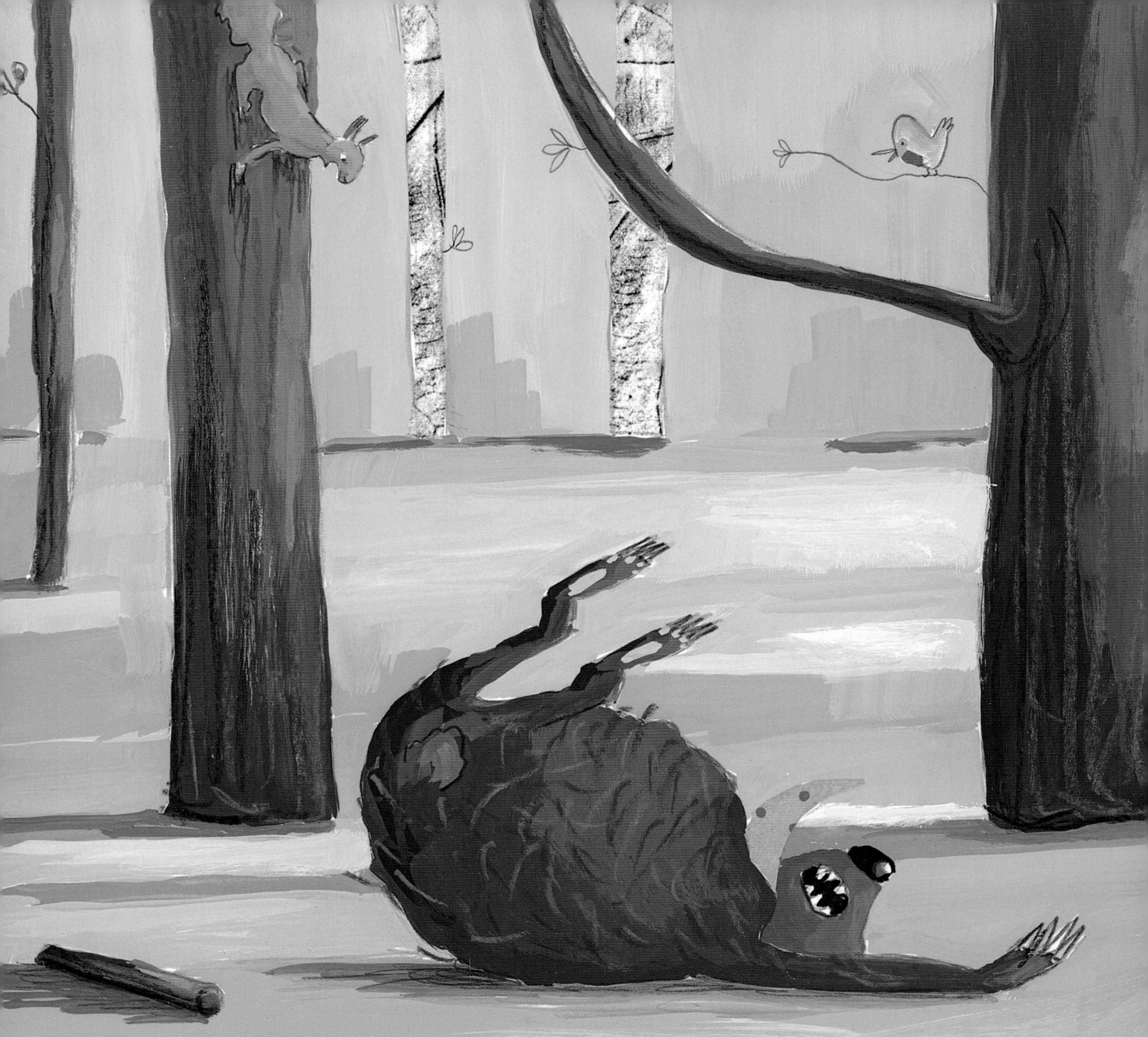

Laughing, Lutz wasn't paying attention and stepped on a stick with his paw.

And *bumm badabum*, he landed flat on the ground. Elliott was shocked and gasped.

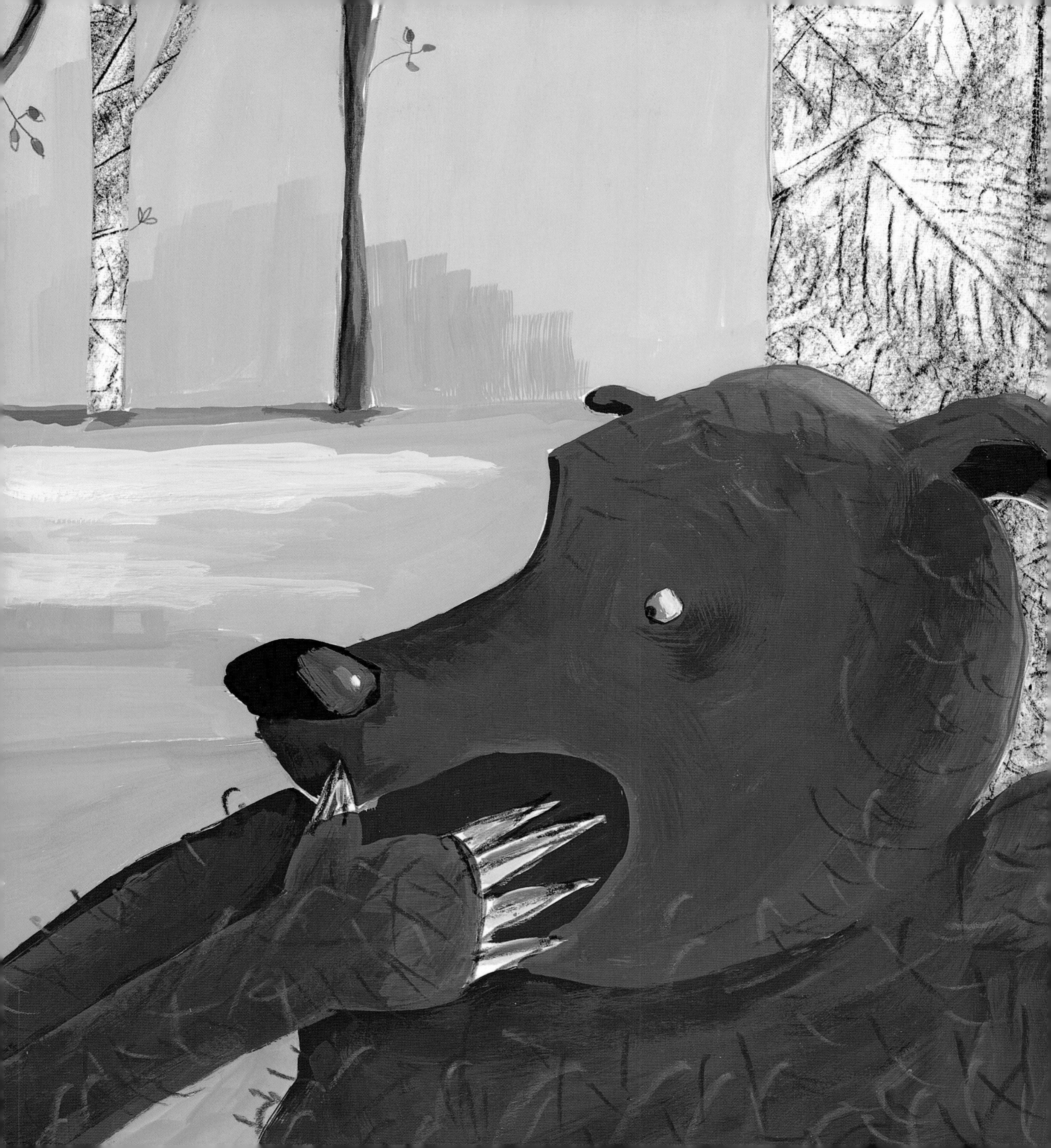

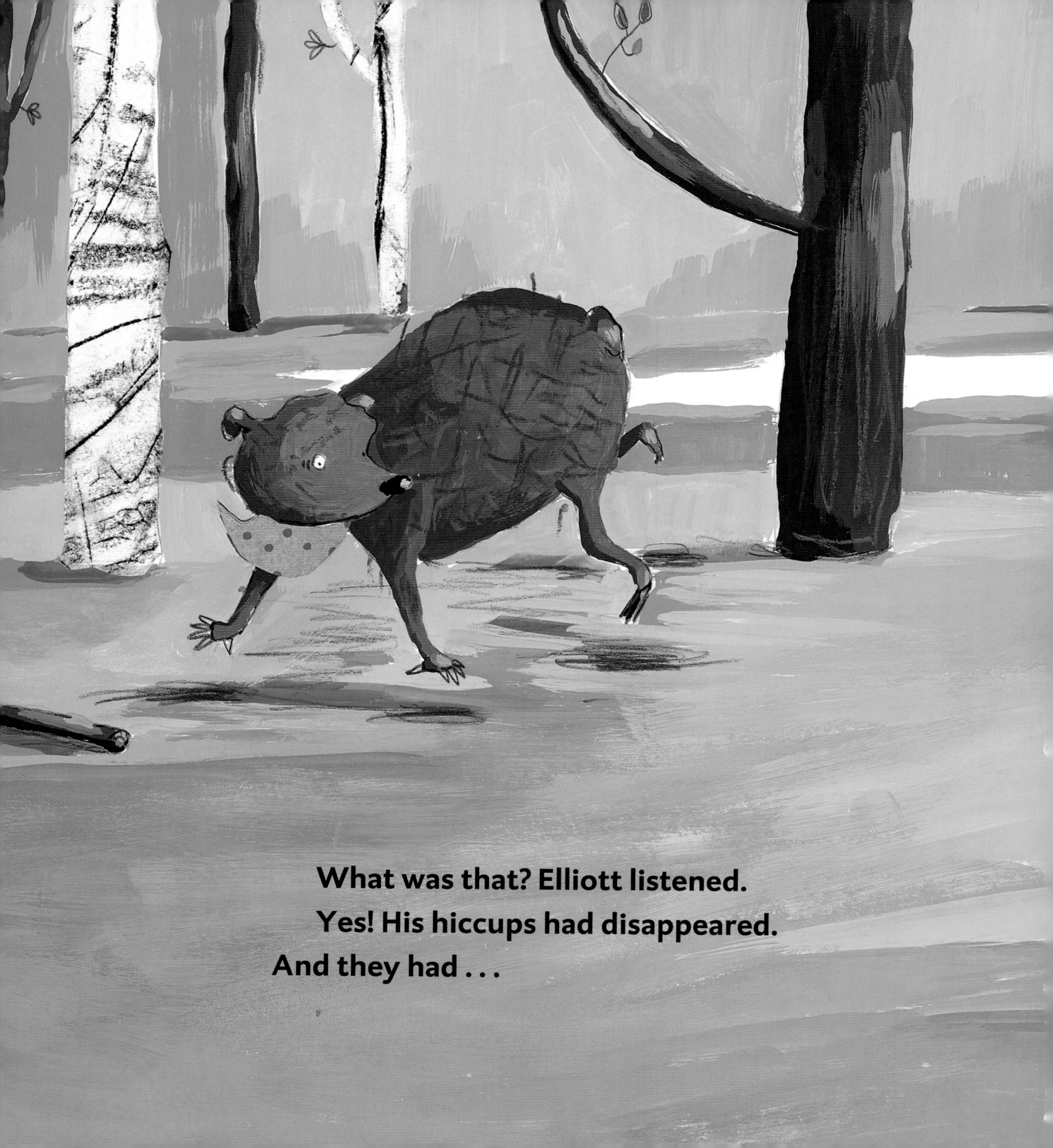

What was that? Elliott listened.
Yes! His hiccups had disappeared.
And they had . . .

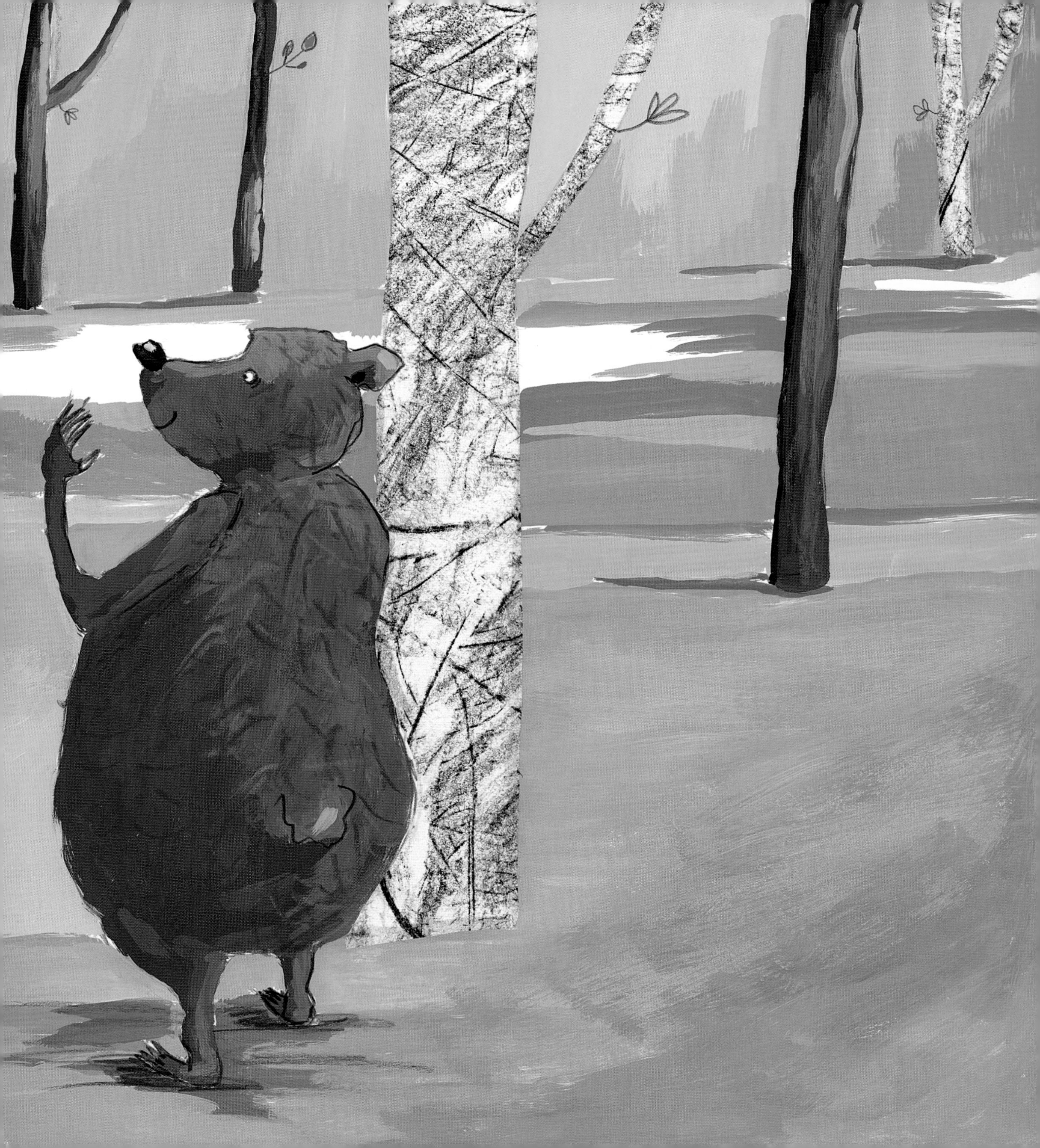

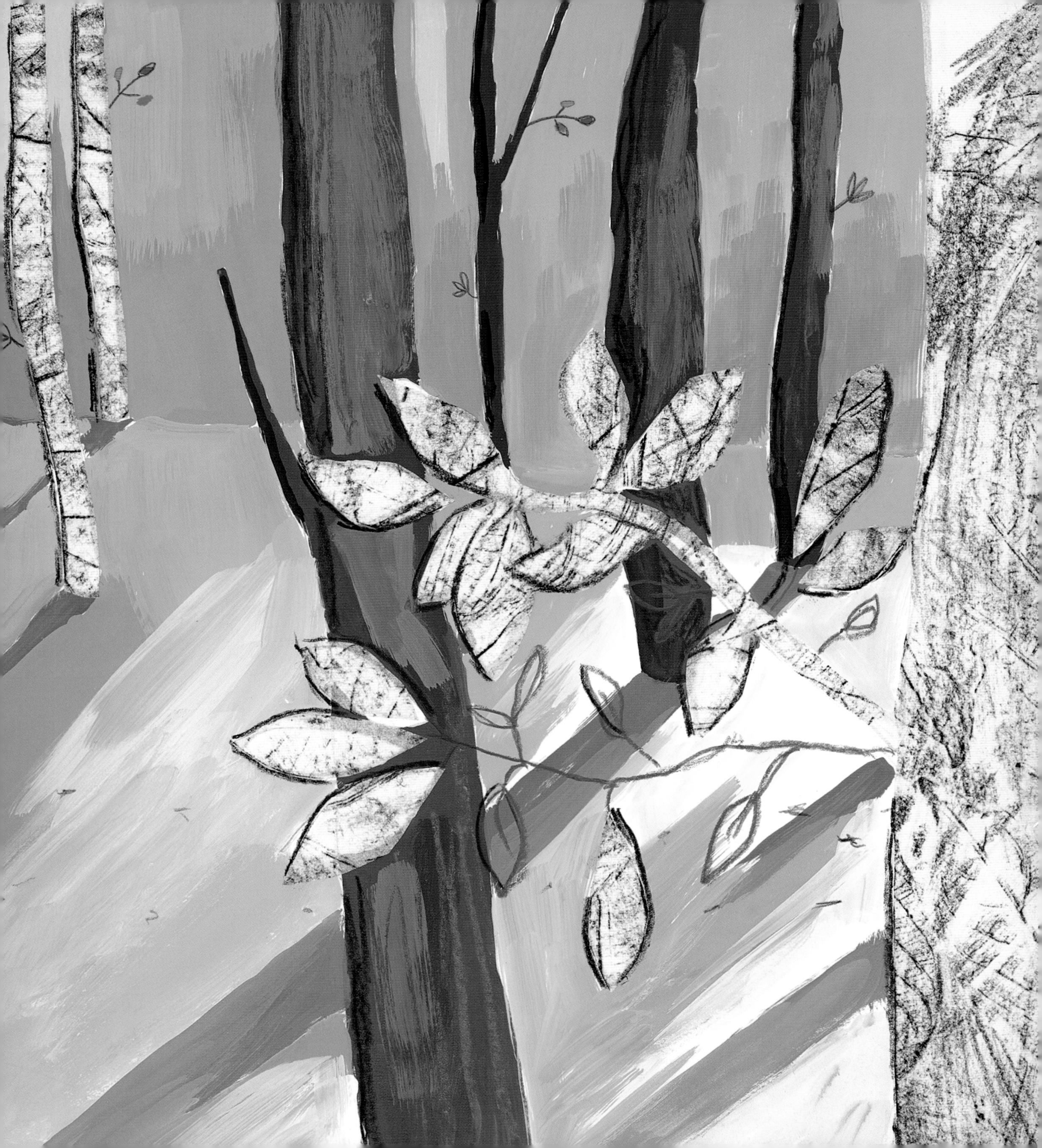

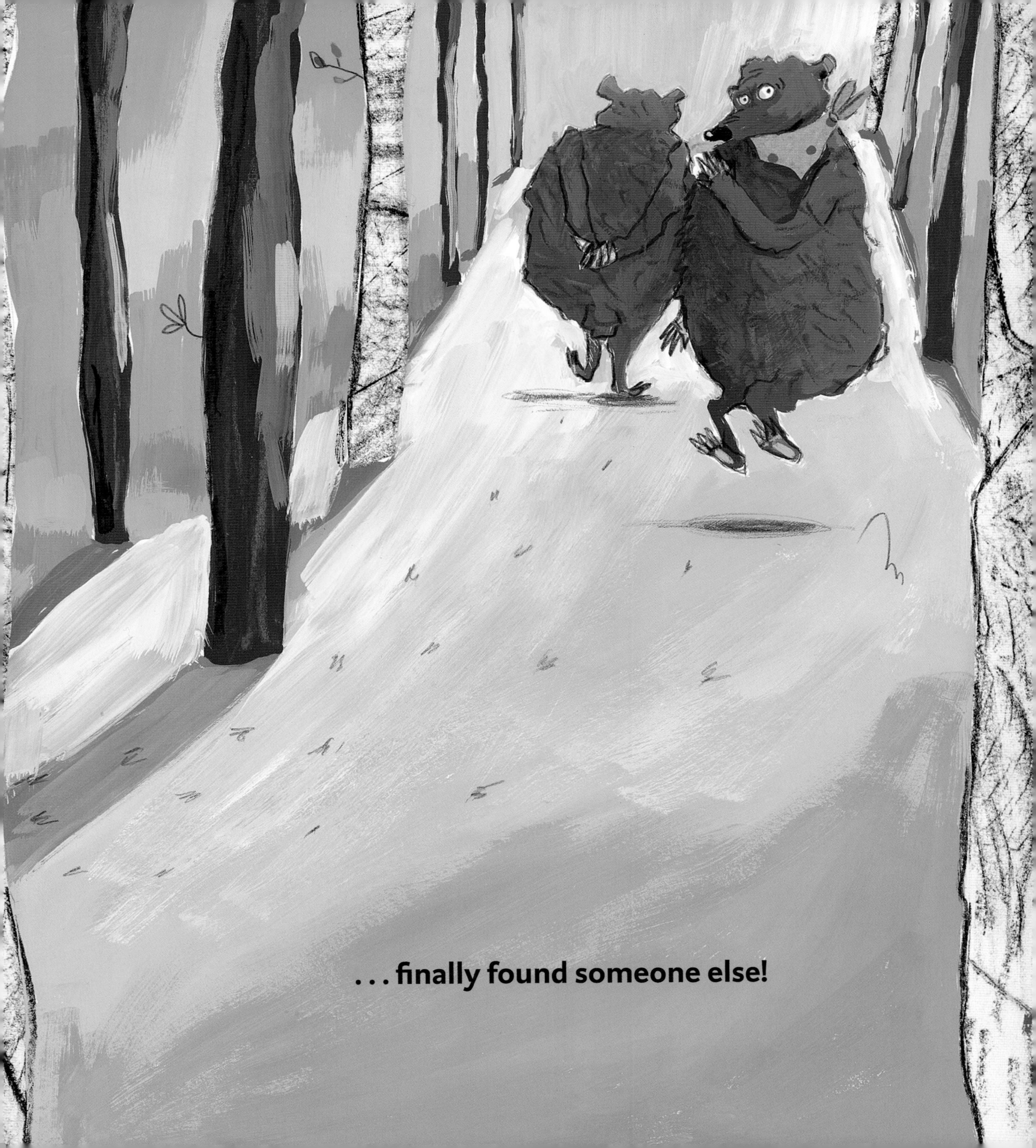

. . . finally found someone else!